Karin's Christmas Walk

KARIN'S CHRISTMAS WALK

by Susan Pearson * pictures by Trinka Hakes Noble

The Dial Press | New York

Published by The Dial Press
1 Dag Hammarskjold Plaza
New York, New York 10017

Library of Congress Cataloging in Publication Data

Pearson, Susan.
Karin's Christmas walk.

SUMMARY | Karin is afraid her favorite uncle
won't arrive in time for Christmas.
[1. Christmas stories. 2. Uncles—Fiction]
I. Noble, Trinka Hakes. II. Title.
PZ7.P323316Kar   [E]   80-11739
ISBN 0-8037-4432-3 (lib. bdg.)
ISBN 0-8037-4431-5

The art for each picture consists of an ink and wash
drawing with two color overlays, all reproduced as halftone.

For Uncle Jerry, of course, with love
SP

For Carlie and The Red Deer
THN

"Karin," Mama called from the kitchen. "I forgot the onions. Be a good girl and run down to Abe's for me."

The snow was falling faster and faster. Karin sighed. "Oh, Mama, can't you send one of the boys?"

"Josh is delivering papers, Peter is practicing, David's not home yet, and Andrew's too little." Mama handed her a five-dollar bill. "Better get a gallon of milk too," she said.

"Oh, all right," Karin answered, pulling on her boots and slipping the money inside her mitten. "It's just not fair," she mumbled. She wanted to be home when Uncle Jerry arrived.

Uncle Jerry was Mama's only brother and Karin's favorite uncle. He was a logger in British Columbia, and they only saw him once a year—at Christmas. Usually he arrived a few days before, but now it was Christmas Eve and he still wasn't here.

The snow crunched under Karin's feet, and she looked up into the sky. There was supposed to be another blizzard tonight. If Uncle Jerry didn't get here soon, he wouldn't make it. And what was Christmas without Uncle Jerry? Nothing, that's what. Just another day.

Mr. Peabody was standing in his front yard feeding the chickadees. He held out his hand filled with birdseed, and they came right up and sat on it while they ate. Mr. Peabody said that's how they fed the birds in St. James's Park in London, England, where he had grown up.

"Hi, Mr. Peabody," Karin called out.

"Well, hello there, Karin," said Mr. Peabody. "Your Uncle Jerry arrived yet?"

"Not yet," Karin answered. "Can I help feed the birds?"

Mr. Peabody filled Karin's mitten with birdseed. When Uncle Jerry came, he always fed the birds with Mr. Peabody too. And he took Karin for walks in the woods. Uncle Jerry knew the names of all the birds and all the trees. They would play a game of who saw what first and who could name what they'd seen. Karin usually won, but she knew that was because Uncle Jerry let her.

Karin tossed the rest of her birdseed on the ground. "I have to go now, Mr. Peabody."

"Well, Merry Christmas, Karin."

"Merry Christmas," Karin answered.

It was snowing a little harder now, Karin thought. She hurried down the street and across Hickory Avenue.

On the corner was Mr. Marzollo's Italian Pastry and Coffee Shop. Uncle Jerry always took Karin and the boys there for lunch. He loved Italian sandwiches.

There weren't many people in Marzollos' today, just a young woman sitting at a table in the window, reading a book. In the woman's lap was a cat. Karin stopped to look. The woman looked up from her book. The cat jumped to the floor. Karin was sorry. The cat looked like Uncle Jerry's tabby, Harold. Uncle Jerry also had a sheep dog named Maude and a bird named Alice-Blue-Gown.

Karin was about to go when the woman knocked on the windowpane. She motioned Karin to bend down. Under the table was the cat. It was feeding four little kittens. Karin watched for a while, then stood up and smiled at the woman. The woman smiled back. They waved good-bye.

Karin went on down the street, across the park, and up the stairs to the railroad station. There were fourteen steps. Karin knew without even counting, because on these steps was where she had learned to count. Mama had taught her before she had even started nursery school.

Once Uncle Jerry had promised her a penny for every number she could say in the right order. When she got to 113, he had laughed and said, "Enough! You're the best counter in the whole world! Tomorrow we're going to the bank and open a savings account for you."

The next day he had taken her to the bank and opened the account. She had gotten a little blue passbook all her own. Uncle Jerry had explained that without even doing anything with the money it would earn more money in the bank and that was called interest. Now when Uncle Jerry came to visit at Christmas, he and Karin always had a banking day when they would go to the bank and have her interest added and Karin would deposit some of her Christmas money.

Karin walked around the railroad station and crossed the street to Abe's. The little bell tinkled as she opened the door.

"Hi, Mr. Rosen," she said.

"Karin! My favorite customer!" Mr. Rosen said. "But what are you doing here on Christmas Eve without your Uncle Jerry?"

"He hasn't come yet," Karin said. "Mama needs a gallon of milk and some onions."

Mr. Rosen put the groceries in a bag and gave her the change. "Don't worry, Karin," he said, "Jerry will make it. He's never missed yet, has he?"

Karin shook her head. Mr. Rosen reached behind him and took a box of chocolates from the shelf. Chocolate was Uncle Jerry's and Karin's favorite candy. He put it in the bag with the onions and the milk. "Tell Uncle Jerry that Abe Rosen says Merry Christmas," he said.

"I will. Thank you, Mr. Rosen," Karin said as she pulled her mittens back on and stuck the change inside one. The bell tinkled again as she went back outside.

Some boys were building a snow fort in the park, but it wasn't nearly as nice as the one Uncle Jerry would build the day after tomorrow when they had their yearly snowball fight. Karin and Mama and Uncle Jerry against Papa and Josh and Peter and David. Andrew was too little to play. He would sit all bundled up on the sled.

Later they would make some clean snowballs. Then Mama would heat maple syrup for sugaring off. When it was ready they dipped the snowballs into it. The hot syrup froze when it hit the cold snow and made a clean maple-syrup candy.

Sugaring off was something Mama and Uncle Jerry had done when they were little—except that they had done it out in the woods with syrup they had made from the sap in the trees. When Mama was little, everyone called her Tom, to go with Jerry. Nobody called Karin anything but Karin, except for Uncle Jerry. He called her Tomassina sometimes.

It was getting dark now and the streetlights had come on. Sally Kelly and her brother and her father were shoveling their walk. "Karin!" Sally called. "Is Uncle Jerry here yet?"

"I don't know," Karin answered. The Kellys' garage door was open, and she could see their bikes hanging on the wall. A few years ago Uncle Jerry had made a surprise visit in the spring, right at the time of the church carnival. Karin had been disappointed when he said he had "important business" and couldn't go with them. There was a wishing well at the carnival, and Mama had asked Karin what she'd wished. "That Uncle Jerry could have come," Karin had said.

"What about that bike you've been wanting?" Mama asked.

"I forgot."

Mama had given her another penny, and Karin had wished for the bike.

When they'd come home, there was a shiny new bike sitting on the front porch, and Karin knew what Uncle Jerry's "important business" had been.

Karin slowed down the last half block to her house. What if he wasn't there yet? What if there was no red pickup outside? She shut her eyes tight. Then she opened them and made herself look in the driveway.

There was the red pickup! Uncle Jerry was here! Karin started to run, but all of a sudden she stopped short. This was the very best time—knowing he was here, knowing that in a few minutes he'd lift her into the air and twirl her around until she was dizzy, and say, "Tomassina! My very own wonderful favorite beautiful niece! I've missed you!"

So instead of racing to the door, Karin walked slowly. The Christmas tree lights were shining in the living room window, and Karin peeked into the room through the boughs of the Christmas tree.

Papa was sitting in Grammie's old Boston rocker with Andrew on his lap. Mama and Uncle Jerry and the boys were on the floor in a circle with books spread open in the middle. Karin knew those books were old family albums. The boys were laughing. They were probably looking at pictures of Mama and Uncle Jerry when they were little and lived in Canada. Uncle Jerry lifted his head and sniffed. He would be smelling the Swedish meatballs cooking. They always had Swedish meatballs on the first night Uncle Jerry was there. That was his favorite, and Mama's and Karin's too.

Now Uncle Jerry put his arm around Mama, and Karin knew he was calling her Tom.

Karin tiptoed across the porch to the front door. She put her hand on the doorknob, but for just one last moment she didn't turn it. For just one last moment they didn't know she was here, but she knew Uncle Jerry was here. For just one last moment she thought, *Next is the very best most wonderful time in the whole year.*

Then she opened the door.

"Tomassina! My very own wonderful favorite beautiful niece! I've missed you!" And Uncle Jerry lifted her high into the air and twirled her around until she was dizzy.

Susan Pearson

is the author of several books for young readers, most recently *Molly Moves Out,* a Dial Easy-to-Read illustrated by Steven Kellogg. Her book *Izzie* was selected as a *New York Times* Outstanding Book of the Year in 1975, and *Monnie Hates Lydia* was an ALA Children's Book of International Interest. Ms. Pearson lives in Minneapolis, Minnesota, where, in addition to writing, she is an editor of children's books.

Trinka Hakes Noble

is the author-illustrator of *The King's Tea,* a Child Study Association Book of the Year, 1979. Ms. Noble grew up in rural southern Michigan and has taught art in Michigan, Virginia, and Rhode Island. She recently studied illustration at Caldecott medalist Uri Shulevitz's workshop. She currently lives in Upper Montclair, New Jersey, with her husband and daughter.

E   (7 DAY-CHRISTMAS)   c.2
Pearson, Susan.
  Karin's Christmas walk
                        8.44

JAN 24 1985